READ with CHIRP

Read Along with Pictures

Every day is an adventure with Chirp!

Owl kids

From the publisher of

chirp chickaDEE OWL

Visit us online!
www.owlkids.com

To my grandson Gavin and granddaughter Rose with love.
— Bob

About the illustrator: Bob Kain brings Chirp to life in every issue of *Chirp Magazine*. Bob's career has included running an animation studio for 30 years, creating newspaper comic strips, and teaching cartooning to kids. His most enthusiastic students these days are his grandchildren.

© 2006 Bayard Canada Books Inc.

Editorial Director: Mary Beth Leatherdale
Designer: Claudia Dávila
Text: Helaine Becker

Publisher: Jennifer Canham
Production Manager: Lesley Zimic

Chirp is a registered trademark of Bayard Presse Canada Inc.

Special thanks to Hilary Bain, Maria Birmingham, Katherine Dearlove, Jackie Farquhar, Angela Keenlyside, Barb Kelly, and Sarah Trusty.

We gratefully acknowledge the financial support of the Government of Canada through the Book Publishing Industry Development Program (BPIDP) for our publishing activities.

Library and Archives Canada Cataloguing in Publication
Kain, Bob, 1932-
Read with Chirp / Bob Kain

ISBN 2-89579-110-4 (bound).--ISBN 2-89579-082-5 (pbk.)

1. Rebuses – Juvenile literature.   I. Title.

PN6371.5. K333 2006   j818'.602   C2005-907287-3

Printed in Canada

Owlkids Publishing
10 Lower Spadina Ave., Suite 400
Toronto, Ontario M5V 2Z2
Ph: 416-340-2700
Fax: 416-340-9769

READ with CHIRP

Read Along with Pictures

Bob Kain

Owl kids

Deep-Sea Treasure

Chirp is on a trip with his friends and and his

dog . Splash! A big rocks the .

"Oh no!" cries . "My favourite ! It fell into the  ."

"Leave it to me!" says brave . "I'll find it."

 dives into the . Down, down, down he goes. Along comes a .

"Hello, !" says . "Did you see a ?"

The points. "Try down there."

Down, down, down goes. He passes an .

"Hello, ! Did you see a 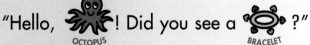 ?"

The points. "Try down there."

Turn the page to see what Chirp finds!

Down, down, down (CHIRP) goes. He passes a (STARFISH).

"Hello, (STARFISH)! Did you see a (BRACELET)?"

"Try the (SHIPWRECK)," says the (STARFISH).

(CHIRP) swims to the (SHIPWRECK). He sees a (TREASURE CHEST) of (COINS). He sees (RINGS) and (NECKLACES). He sees sparkling (DIAMONDS). But where is (TWEET)'s (BRACELET)?

There it is! It's in the (TREASURE CHEST)!

Up, up, up (CHIRP) goes. "Thank you, (STARFISH)!"

Up, up, up (CHIRP) goes. "Thank you, (OCTOPUS)!"

Up, up, up (CHIRP) goes. "Thank you, (FISH)!"

"Surprise!" says (CHIRP) as he splashes out of the water. "I have (PRESENTS)!"

He gives a shiny (DIAMOND) to (SQUAWK). He gives a beautiful jewelled (COLLAR) to (SPARKY).

"But what about me?" asks (TWEET).

(CHIRP) gives (TWEET) her lost (BRACELET), and (TWEET) gives (CHIRP) a big (BEAR) hug!

Safari Adventure

Chirp and  SPARKY are on an African safari. **2** great big 👀 EYES stare

at them from behind a 🌳 TREE.

"Who's there?" asks 🦉 CHIRP.

"It's just me!" yawns a 🦁 LION. "Would you like to stay and chat?"

"No, thanks," says 🦉 CHIRP. " 🐶 SPARKY and I have to go. We're on a safari!"

🦉 CHIRP and 🐶 SPARKY trek through the tall ⋀⋀⋀ GRASS until they see a big 〰️ RIVER.

It's filled with hungry 🐊 CROCODILES. How will they get across?

"Leave it to me, 🐶 SPARKY! Grab on," shouts 🦉 CHIRP as he reaches for a

hanging 🌿 VINE. "Wheeeee!" They swing across the river.

"Woof!" 🐶 SPARKY thanks 🦉 CHIRP when they are safely on the other side.

"No problemo," 🦉 CHIRP says. "That's what friends are for." ●

12

Soccer Star

His lucky number is _____.

Chirp loves to play

_____.

Look at the pictures and say the missing words.

Chirp _____ down the soccer field.

He moves the ball with his _____.

He kicks the _____.

The ball goes into the _____.

Hooray, Chirp scored a _____!

A Super Snack

"I'm hungry. Let's make sandwiches!" suggests .

"Yuck," says 's friend . "I don't like sandwiches!

How about and ?"

"I don't like and or sandwiches," sniffs 's friend .

"Then what are we going to eat?" asks . "My tummy is rumbling!"

"How about some 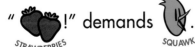?" pleads . "Everyone likes tasty ."

 says, " are OK. But I like juicy better."

" !" insists .

" 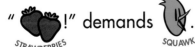!" demands .

"Hey guys," says . "Let's choose a snack we all like!"

Turn the page to see Chirp's idea!

SQUAWK thinks. TWEET thinks. CHIRP thinks.

"Leave it to me!" says CHIRP. "I know exactly what to make!"

CHIRP gets a large BOWL. He gets a KNIFE and an APRON.

He puts on his CHEF'S HAT!

CHIRP washes the STRAWBERRIES. He puts them into the BOWL. SQUAWK is very happy.

CHIRP slices the BANANAS. The BANANAS go into the BOWL, too. Now TWEET is happy.

Next, CHIRP gets some GRAPES and an APPLE from the FRIDGE. He washes the GRAPES

and puts them into the BOWL with the STRAWBERRIES and the BANANAS.

Now it's time to wash the APPLE. Then CHIRP slices the APPLE.

Into the BOWL it goes. What is the snack?

CHIRP's yummy FRUIT SALAD, of course! ●

18

Sky-High Games

Chirp is tucked into BED. But CHIRP is not sleepy.

 CHIRP goes outside and sees the MOON winking down at him.

"I bet the MOON wants to play," thinks CHIRP. So CHIRP gets his magic CAPE.

Up, up, and away. SUPERCHIRP is off to outer space!

Along the way, SUPERCHIRP meets some friendly STARS who want to

play tag. "You're It, SUPERCHIRP!" they call.

 SUPERCHIRP tries to catch the STARS, but they are too fast for him.

They decide to play RING around the ROSE **E** instead.

Then SUPERCHIRP has another idea: "Let's play hopscotch!" he says.

Hip! Hop! Hip! Hop! SUPERCHIRP skips from PLANET to PLANET.

Turn the page to see what other games they play!

"Would you like to play catch?" asks a ⭐ (STAR). "The ☀️ (SUN) can be the ⚾ (BALL)!" The ⭐ (STAR) tosses the ☀️ (SUN) to 🐦 (SUPERCHIRP).

"Ouch! Ouch! Ouch! The ☀️ (SUN) is too hot!" shrieks 🐦 (SUPERCHIRP).

"We can't play with the ☀️ (SUN) or we'll get a ☀️ (SUN) - burn!"

"It's getting late," says the 🌙 (MOON). "It's time for us all to go back 🏠 (HOME)."

The littlest ⭐ (STAR) starts to 😢 (CRY). "I don't know where to go!"

Another ⭐ (STAR) starts to 😢 (CRY). "Me neither."

"Leave it to me!" shouts 🐦 (SUPERCHIRP). He grabs the ⭐⭐ (STARS), whirls around, and sends them spinning back 🏠 (HOME).

"Thanks a million!" the ⭐⭐ (STARS) cheer.

"🐦 (SUPERCHIRP), you're a super-⭐ (STAR)," winks the 🌙 (MOON). ●

Down on the Farm

The farm animals are hungry for their breakfast.

"Leave it to me!" says . Chirp gets out a of food.

" , breakfast!" he calls. comes, wagging his .

Next come the . feeds them their yummy food!

But there are still more animals to feed.

 goes to the  . In the , there are and .

 gives to the and fresh to the .

Then goes up to the green . In the , there are

 . brings them all of .

Now the ,  , , and are fed.

What's the next job for ?

Turn the page to see what Chirp's next job is!

 gets a big thank you from all of his farm friends! ●